My Very First Winnie the Pooh™

Singing Nursery Rhymes with Pooh

Compiled by Cassandra Case

GROLIER
B O O K S

BOOK CLUB EDITION

Based on the Pooh stories by A.A. Milne
(copyright The Pooh Properties Trust).

Printed in the United States of America.

First published by Disney Press, New York, NY
This edition published by Grolier Books, ISBN: 0-7172-8894-3
Grolier Books is a division of Grolier Enterprises, Inc.

"Christopher Robin got up very early one morning. The sun came shining through the Hundred-Acre Wood as it climbed up into the sky.

He thought it was probably too early to wake any of his friends, so Christopher Robin stretched out under a tree.

He wanted to think up a new,
fun game that he and his friends
could play today.

Suddenly, he heard a giggle.

Christopher Robin looked around and discovered Tigger holding one of Piglet's feet.

"Oh, hello! What are you doing?" asked Christopher Robin.

"I'm doing the piggy-foot rhyme," said Tigger, "but Piglet's piggy-feet are very wiggly!"

"I know the rhyme you mean!" cried Christopher Robin. So he and Tigger said it together:

this Little Piggy

This little piggy went to market,
and this little piggy stayed home;
This little piggy had roast beef,
and this little piggy had none;
And this little piggy cried.
Wee, wee, wee, all the way home.

"You're tickling me!" Piglet giggled.

"**t**his gives me an idea for a game!" said Christopher Robin. "Let's see how many rhymes we can remember. But first, let's go see if Pooh Bear wants to play, too."

Pooh was still sound asleep. So they sang rather loudly:

Are You Sleeping?

Are you sleeping, are you sleeping,
Brother John, Brother John?
Morning bells are ringing,
Morning bells are ringing.
Ding, ding, dong.
Ding, ding, dong.

First – of course – Pooh had to have break-fast. While he ate, he joined in the game. When his mouth was full, he hummed. But mostly, in a sticky sort of voice, he recited:

Little Jack Horner

Little Jack Horner sat in a corner,
Eating his Christmas pie.
He stuck in his thumb and pulled out a plum,
And said, "What a good boy am I."

Pease Porridge Hot

Pease porridge hot, pease porridge cold,
Pease porridge in the pot, nine days old.
Some like it hot, some like it cold,
Some like it in the pot, nine days old.

then the friends went out to see who else wanted to play. As they were about to cross a field, Piglet sang this song:

Baa Baa Black Sheep

Baa baa black sheep, have you any wool?
Yes, sir, yes, sir, three bags full.
One for my master, one for the dame,
And one for the little boy who lives down the lane.

When they got to the other side of the field, there was Christopher Robin's see-saw. Pooh and Piglet sat right down to sing:

See Saw, Margery Daw

See saw, Margery Daw,
*   Johnny shall have a new master.*
He shall have but a penny a day
*   because he can't work any faster.*

Singing songs and walking along, Pooh, Piglet, Christopher Robin, and Tigger came to Rabbit's garden. Without even stopping to think, Rabbit remembered two garden rhymes to sing for them:

Mary, Mary,
Quite Contrary

Mary, Mary, quite contrary,
How does your garden grow?
"With silver bells and cockle shells
And pretty maids all in a row."

Oats, Peas, Beans

Oats, peas, beans, and barley grow;
Oats, peas, beans, and barley grow;
Do you or I or anyone know
How oats, peas, beans, and
*   barley grow?*

"**B**ushes are vegibbles, aren't they?" cried Tigger. "I know one about a bush . . . and we go round, an' round, an' round!"

Everyone joined hands in a circle, singing:

Here We Go Round the Mulberry Bush

Here we go 'round the mulberry bush,
the mulberry bush, the mulberry bush.
Here we go 'round the mulberry bush,
so early in the morning.

t

heard
rhyme

Ring Around the Rosy

Ring around the rosy,
A pocket full of posies.
Ashes, ashes,
We all fall down.

Just then, Owl flew over to say that Eeyore was still fast asleep. So they all trooped off to find Eeyore and wake him with this song:

Lazy Mary

Lazy Mary, will you get up,
Will you get up,
Will you get up?
Lazy Mary, will you get up,
Will you get up this
    morning?

By now, Pooh was getting rumbly in the tumbly. He invited everyone to his house and sure enough, when they got there, they were just in time for a smackerel!

Looking at the clock made Pooh think of this rhyme:

Hickory, Dickory, Dock

Hickory, dickory, dock!
The mouse ran up the clock.
The clock struck one,
The mouse ran down,
Hickory, dickory, dock!

With help from Piglet, Pooh cooked up something yummy. As they stirred, they sang these songs:

Pat-a-Cake

Pat-a-cake, pat-a-cake, baker's man,
Bake me a cake as fast as you can.
Pat it and roll it and mark it with a B,
And put it in the oven for baby and me.

Muffin Man

Do you know the muffin man,
*   the muffin man,*
*   the muffin man?*
Do you know the muffin man
*   who lives on Drury Lane?*
Yes I know the muffin man,
*   the muffin man,*
*   the muffin man.*
Yes I know the muffin man,
*   who lives on Drury lane.*

While the muffins were baking, the friends put on a musical show with this rhyme:

Old King Cole

Old King Cole was a merry old soul,
And a merry old soul was he.
He called for his pipe and he called for his bowl,
And he called for his fiddlers three.

When Pooh and his guests finished eating, it was raining, so they got their rain-gear and ran outside singing:

It's Raining, It's Pouring

It's raining, it's pouring,
The old man is snoring.
He went to bed
And bumped his head,
And didn't wake up
*   till morning.*

After the rain stopped, they played boats in the puddles and acted out two of Piglet's favorite rhymes:

Row, Row, Row Your Boat

Row, row, row your boat
Gently down the stream.
Merrily, merrily, merrily, merrily.
Life is but a dream.

Rub-a-dub-dub

Rub-a-dub-dub, three men in a tub,
And who do you think they be?
The butcher, the baker,
    the candlestick maker.
Turn them out, knaves all three.

edtime came, but Roo and Tigger were having too much fun bouncing and saying this rhyme over and over:

Jack Be Nimble

Jack be nimble,
Jack be quick,
Jack jump over the candlestick.

Then Owl said he would sing a song his mama used to sing when he was little, so Roo settled right down to listen to this lullaby:

Rock-a-Bye Baby

Rock-a-bye baby, in the tree top,
When the wind blows, the cradle will rock.
When the bough breaks, the cradle will fall,
And down will come baby, cradle, and all.

On their way home, Pooh and Piglet looked up into the dark sky and sang:

twinkle, twinkle, Little Star

Twinkle, twinkle, little star
How I wonder what you are.
Up above the world so high,
Like a diamond in the sky.
Twinkle, twinkle, little star
How I wonder what you are.

Then they each made a happy wish for tomorrow.